Tyler has TONSILLITIS

TONSILS

- Soft Palate
- Tonsils
- Uvula
- Tongue

Tate Publishing & Enterprises

a story by **Rick Saupé, MD**

Published by Tate Publishing & Enterprises, LLC
127 E. Trade Center Terrace | Mustang, Oklahoma 73064 USA
1.888.361.9473 | www.tatepublishing.com

Tate Publishing is committed to excellence in the publishing industry. The company reflects the philosophy established by the founders, based on Psalm 68:11,
"The Lord gave the word and great was the company of those who published it."

Book design copyright © 2011 by Tate Publishing, LLC. All rights reserved.
Cover and interior design by Scott Parrish
Illustrations by Kathy Hoyt

Published in the United States of America

ISBN: 978-1-61777-763-9
Juvenile Fiction / Animals / Lions, Tigers, Leopards, Etc.
11.05.17

Dedication

To Ella and Heidi, for their enduring support and enthusiasm for this story, and to Penny, for encouraging me to tell it.

Acknowledgements

I wish to sincerely thank all of my mentors, colleagues, and patients, past and present, for teaching me everything I know about the art and science of anesthesiology.

Introduction

This book is written for, inspired by, and dedicated to the thousands of children who undergo the experience of surgery and anesthesia every year. Whether they are going through it for the first time, or the fifteenth, having surgery is an anxiety-provoking experience, both for the child as well as—if not more—for the parents. Medicine is both an art and a science, and nowhere is the "art" of medicine more apparent than in the practice of caring for young children. The entire surgical experience can be made or broken by the preoperative interaction with the anesthesia care team, usually in the few minutes prior to entering the operating room.

As the father of two young children, I have learned to appreciate the calming effect of a lighthearted, relevant story when confronted by a new and/or intimidating experience. To the parents and caregivers, I hope you find this book both informative and useful when dealing with your child's surgical experience. One of the most difficult things to do as a parent is to surrender the care of your child to another person when they (and you) are most vulnerable. As anesthesiologists, our job is to make this experience as painless as possible, both physically and emotionally, for everyone involved.

While this particular story may not be completely relevant to your child's planned operation, the general flow of the experience represented by Tyler Tiger's tonsillectomy is applicable and adaptable to a variety of situations.

Good luck and stay calm. The anticipation is usually worse than the actual event.

Tyler Tiger was *not* having a good day. He woke up in the morning with a headache and yet another sore throat.

"Dad," he asked, "can I stay home from school today?" "But, Tyler," said his dad, "you've already stayed home from school twice this month. Try eating some breakfast and maybe you'll feel better."

But Tyler wasn't hungry, and every time he took a drink of his juice, it hurt his throat to swallow.

Mrs. Tiger placed her paw on Tyler's forehead. "Let's take your temperature," she said. "If you have a fever, I'll let you stay home to rest."

Tyler's mom shook her head. "Well, Ty, your temperature *is* a little high, so you probably should stay home. But first, I think we should go see Dr. Duckworth."

Tyler didn't feel like seeing the doctor, but he always got to pick out a sticker on his way out of the office, and Tyler loved stickers.

In the waiting room, Tyler flipped through a picture book.

After a few minutes, Nurse Ella came out and called, "Tyler Tiger...the doctor will see you now."

Tyler and his mom followed Nurse Ella into a smaller room, where she took his temperature and measured how tall he was. Dr. Duckworth waddled in and looked at Tyler. He listened to his heart, looked in his ears, and finally looked in his mouth with a special light. "Open up and say ahh…"

Tyler opened his mouth.

"Hmm ...looks like we found the problem," quacked the doctor. "You've got tonsillitis."

"Tonsil-*what*-is?" asked Tyler.

"Tonsillitis," explained the doctor. "It means your tonsils are a lot bigger than they should be. You see, Ty, your tonsils sit in the back of your throat, right behind your tongue. Normal tonsils look pink, like this, but sometimes when you get sick, your tonsils can get BIG and RED and **SWOLLEN** and can make it hard to breathe and swallow. When that happens, you might feel better if we took them out."

TONSILS

Soft Palate

Tonsils

Uvula

Tongue

Dr. Duckworth glanced over at Tyler's mom. "You said this is his third sore throat this month? It might be time to think about a tonsillectomy. Let's give it a few days and see how he feels. If the tonsils are still big, we'll plan on doing surgery at the end of the week, okay?"

Tyler was unusually quiet on the way home.

"Mom," he finally asked, "what's 'surgery'?"

"Surgery is when you go to the hospital and the doctor fixes something that's wrong with you," she explained. "Hopefully you won't need surgery, but if you do, they give you something called anesthesia, which makes you go to sleep, and when it's all over, you wake up."

"But won't it hurt?" he asked.

"Actually, when they give you the anesthesia you won't feel a thing. I had my tonsils out when I was little, and it really wasn't that bad."

When they got home, Tyler went to his room and played with his toys for the rest of the day.

At the end of the week, they went back to see Dr. Duckworth. His throat was feeling better, and his growl started sounding normal again.

"Let's see those tonsils, little buddy," said Dr. Duckworth. Tyler opened his mouth wide.

"Hmm," said the doctor, "your tonsils still look pretty swollen. I guess they'll need to come out. We can schedule your surgery for tomorrow morning."

The doctor could tell that Tyler was a little scared, so he sat down next to him and wrapped his wing around him. "Don't worry, Tyler. Everything will be just fine, and we'll have you roaring again in no time. Now go have a yummy dinner tonight because you can't eat anything before surgery tomorrow."

Tyler and his parents went to the Pizza Shack that night, and Tyler ate two slices of pizza and an ice cream cone.

"Mom and Dad," he said, while licking his ice cream, "can you come into surgery with me?"

"We can't stay with you *during* the surgery," answered his mom, "but we'll be there until you go to sleep, and we'll be there when you wake up, okay?"

"Okay," said Tyler. "As long as you're with me, I'll be okay."

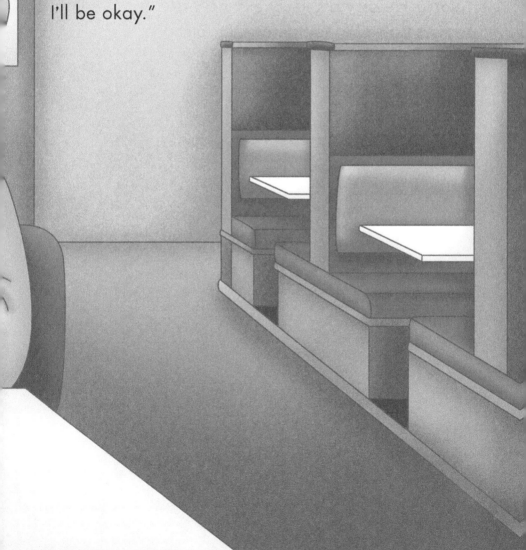

The next morning, the Tigers arrived at Jungleview Hospital.

"You must be Tyler Tiger!" said one of the nurses, handing him some pajamas. "My name is Heidi, but my friends call me Hoppy." She reached into her pouch and pulled out a pair of soft, fuzzy slippers. "And these will keep your paws warm while you're asleep."

Nurse Heidi walked Tyler and his parents down to the operating room, where they met the anesthesiologist.

"Hi, Tyler, I'm Dr. Snow! My job is to take care of you while you're sleeping. If you like, one of your parents can come with you, and they can hold your paw while you drift off to sleep."

"I'll go," said Mr. Tiger, "and your mom and I will be waiting for you when you wake up."

"Now," said Dr. Snow, "when it's time for you to go to sleep, I need your help blowing up a balloon with a special mask. Do you think you can handle that?"

"Oh, I can handle it!" roared Tyler.

"That's the spirit, little buddy! Now, would you like some medicine to relax you before surgery? It's cherry-flavored."

"Okay," said Tyler. The medicine tasted a little funny, but it made him feel a lot less nervous about the surgery.

A few minutes later, Tyler and his dad followed Dr. Snow into a room filled with lots of lights and machines and TV screens.

"This is the operating room," explained Dr. Snow, "and each time you breathe through your mask, this balloon will get bigger, and you'll slowly drift off to sleep. When you wake up, your tonsils will be gone, and so will all those sore throats you've been having."

Tyler lay down on the bed, and Dr. Snow put a
little clip on his finger that had a red light inside.

"This light measures your heartbeat," he explained,
"and that beeping sound you hear is *your* heart,
Tyler."

Tyler's dad held his paw. As he started breathing
through the mask, he suddenly felt very sleepy and
was having trouble keeping his eyes open.

"Tyler. Tyler. Time to wake up, honey."

Tyler opened his eyes, but the room looked very different than the one he was in before. His mouth was dry, and his throat was a little sore, but otherwise he felt pretty well.

"Where am I?" he whispered.

"You're in the recovery room, Tyler. It's me, Nurse Hoppy—I mean Heidi—and your surgery is all done."

Tyler sat right up. "It's over? Really?" He couldn't believe his ears. "Where are my parents?"

"They'll be here in a minute," said the nurse. "While you're waiting, can I get you a Popsicle? It will help your throat feel better."

"Can I have a green one?" he whispered.

"Green it is!" said the nurse.

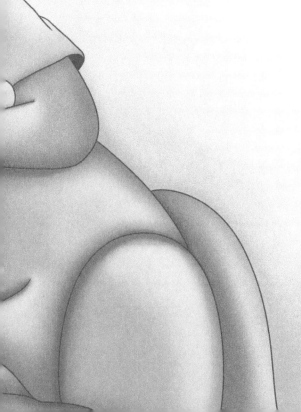

Tyler started to smile when his mom and dad walked into the room.

"How are you feeling, kiddo?" his mom asked, kissing him on the forehead.

"My throat's a little sore, but I'm just so glad it's over," said Tyler.

"So are we, sweetie. So are we."

Later that day, Tyler and his parents got in the car to drive home.

"You know," he said, "that wasn't as bad as I thought it would be. And I got to eat a Popsicle for breakfast!"

"See, Tyler? We told you everything would be okay," said his dad. "Now let's go home and we can all relax. I think there's another Popsicle in the freezer with *your* name on it."

Historical Note

Dr. John Snow (1813–1858) was one of the first physicians to specialize in the study of anesthesia. He was famously known for personally providing chloroform anesthesia for Queen Victoria during the birth of two of her children, opening the door for the use of anesthetics to control the pain of childbirth. He was not a polar bear.

the end.

listen|imagine|view|experience

AUDIO BOOK DOWNLOAD INCLUDED WITH THIS BOOK!

In your hands you hold a complete digital entertainment package. Besides purchasing the paper version of this book, this book includes a free download of the audio version of this book. Simply use the code listed below when visiting our website. Once downloaded to your computer, you can listen to the book through your computer's speakers, burn it to an audio CD or save the file to your portable music device (such as Apple's popular iPod) and listen on the go!

How to get your free audio book digital download:

1. Visit www.tatepublishing.com and click on the e|LIVE logo on the home page.
2. Enter the following coupon code:
   4540-fc23-8baa-5469-a5ba-9f3d-e548-2e77
3. Download the audio book from your e|LIVE digital locker and begin enjoying your new digital entertainment package today!

CPSIA information can be obtained at www.ICGtesting.com
Printed in the USA
BVOW11s1135290315

393796BV00008B/17/P